Conestance, Conerad, Cone-Vera and Conen were tired of standing in a line. It was a lovely sunny day: the sort of day which makes you want to go out and have an adventure!

"I'm fed up of standing about," Conen said, "let's go and see what we can find."

"Good idea," Conerad agreed. Conestance and Cone-Vera both smiled and nodded.

The four friends found a gate which opened onto a lovely wooded path.

"Smell the trees and the new grass," Conestance said. "It's so lovely to be away from all the traffic and noise. Let's see where this path goes to." So they got in a line and woggled away into the woods.

A stream sparkled along the side of the path. In the distance they could see a small tunnel.

"I wonder where that goes to," said Conen.

"I don't know," Cone-Vera said, pointing at the sky, "but just look at those big black clouds, it's going to rain. Quickly everyone, let's shelter in there."

As they reached the edge of the tunnel, there was a huge flash of lightning and the loudest thunderclap they had ever heard. "Come on! Get inside out of the rain," Conerad said, pushing the others into the tunnel. "Go on, further in. We need to keep dry."

"**Hello!**" Said a loud voice. "Hello... hello... hello!" came back the echo.

"Oh dear, there are lots of humans in the tunnel! Everyone become Just Cones!" Cone-Vera said, and the friends became Just Cones, no faces, no voices, no hands, no movements: Just Cones.

"Hello, it's me, Conefluence, the water safety Cone!" said a cheery voice.

There was a splish-splashing sound
as Coneflucence arrived. "What are you
doing in the Culvert?"

The four friends saw a Cone with a
hard hat and orange high-visibility
coat looking at them.

"What is a Culvert?" Cone-Vera asked.

"It takes the water away to help stop roads and buildings flooding.
The water is getting much deeper, we must go," Coneflucence explained.
The Cones saw that the water was up over their bases. "Follow me."

They woggled slowly for a very long way. The water got higher and higher as they went. Conefluence shouted, "come on, quickly." The Cones followed him and were shocked by what they saw. They thought the Culvert would take them somewhere safe, but no. They were at the side of a raging river and the water in the Culvert was pouring into it.

"We must get into that boat and get away from here or we'll be swept away by the river," Conefluence yelled. He grabbed hold of the boat and the four Cones scrambled to get in.

"Help! I can't get up!" Cone-Vera shouted, lying on her back in the bottom of the boat, waving her umbrella.

"Ooooh! The way this boat moves makes me feel sick!" Conestance cried.

The boat made it safely across the river to the other side. The five Cones climbed over the side and flopped onto the grass.

"That was close!" Conerad said.

Conefluence looked sternly at the Cones and said, "I hope you have all learned a very important lesson."

"**NEVER** walk into a Culvert. Culverts are part of the flood defences. Flood water escapes safely so that houses and shops don't get flooded. You saw how quickly the water rose in the storm; it only takes a few minutes to get into serious trouble. You could all have been drowned or washed away and lost."

The four friends were pleased to be safe. "Rivers and canals are dangerous when there is a flood," Conefluence explained. "If you want to enjoy some time near water, go onto the river-side path or go over the bridge to the canal. These are beautiful places to walk with lots of interesting things to see. Go on, have some fun; just be careful near the banks."

Conestance, Conerad, Cone-Vera and Conen looked at each other. "I think I've seen enough water," Conestance said and the others nodded in agreement.

"Let's go find somewhere we can watch what those humans are doing down there," Conerad said. "With all that machinery, it must be interesting."

As nightfall came, it stopped raining and all the workmen went home. Big security lights illuminated the workings.

"Look at all that machinery! Let's go and explore," Conen said.

"Better not," Cone-Vera said and pointed to the night security guard. "We'll wait for Conefluence tomorrow; we don't want to risk being stacked."

Next morning, Conefluence woggled up and said, "hello again! What are you doing?" Cone-Vera explained that they wanted to see what the humans were making. "This is most important," Conefluence said proudly. "The humans are making flood defences to help protect their buildings and roads from flooding and water damage. Put these hi-viz coats on and I'll show you."

Very carefully they picked their way towards the workings. "This is a very deep river so the workers must be careful," Coneflluence explained. "The humans are below the water level here. This is called a Cofferdam. It keeps humans safe while they build this big construction called a weir. The weir can be raised and lowered if floods come. It lets the water flow safely and helps to avoid flooding."

"Look at all that rubbish floating over there," Conefluence pointed. "Some humans are very naughty and throw all kinds of things into the river which makes it dangerous for both boats and water creatures. Rubbish also blocks the river and makes flooding worse."

"As well as making the river safer for themselves, the humans are also making it better for the river creatures. Can you see that slim channel over there? It is needed so that water creatures called eels can swim up the river, and the wider channel is for fish and otters to swim up as well," Coneflunce explained.

"Amazing!" Cone-Vera said.

Conefluence smiled and pointed. "Look, over there by the entrance to the culvert. Those are otters, wonderful, pretty creatures, which are nesting nearby. There are beautiful fish called salmon who come chasing up the river to lay their eggs further up-stream. These creatures only like to live in clean water."

Cone-Vera, Conerad and Conen spent some time looking around the works and machinery with Conefluence, while Conestance sat on the grass and enjoyed her surroundings and the sunshine. Some beautiful swans flew overhead and landed on the canal, fluffing up their feathers and dabbling for weed to eat.

Conestance was thrilled with the swans and wanted the others to see them. She waved her handbag to get their attention and very soon they woggled over to where she was resting.

"What have you seen?" Cone-Vera asked.

Conestance pointed to the swans, "aren't they just the most beautiful things? Let's go closer."

"Just wait a minute," Conefluence said. "Swans are beautiful, but you see the ones with brown feathers? They are babies and their parents are very protective. They'll hit you with their wings if you go too close and you'll get really hurt."

"Enjoy your woggle but do be careful of the Giant Hogweed,"
Conefluence said, pointing to very tall plants with tiny white flowers.
  "They're taller than humans!" Cone-Vera gasped.
  "If you touch them," Conefluence explained, "they will make your skin
sensitive to sunlight, it will blister and you could be scarred for life.
Humans must go to hospital if they touch it."

The four friends promised to be careful and waved 'goodbye' to Conefluence. A canal boat came towards them on the canal. The Cones became 'Just Cones' so the humans wouldn't see them. As they passed the Cones, a human threw a bag full of rubbish into the water.

"That is so naughty!" Conestance exclaimed.

"We can't leave it there," Cone-Vera said, frowning. "Remember what Conefluence said about the trouble rubbish causes. Perhaps one of us should go into the water and get it out."

"Don't look at me," Conestance said. "I really, really don't like getting wet!"

The friends stood on the grass at the side of the canal, wondering what to do. "Conefluence will find someone to get that rubbish out," Conestance said. "We can't reach it." They all woggled farther onto the grass and nearer to the edge of the canal. There was a loud splash. Conerad had gone too far and fallen off the grass into the water!

Conerad's head popped up. "Quickly, get out of the water," Cone-Vera said.

"Help me, I can't!" Conerad cried.

"Give us your hands and we'll pull you out," Conerad said.

However hard they pulled, they couldn't get Conerad onto dry land.

Conefluence came up the path. He saw Conerad in the water, picked up a life buoy and threw it to him. "Sorry! Forgot to tell you! Canal banks are steep and straight-sided. Grass hangs over – you can't see where the path ends and water begins. Getting out is nearly impossible if you fall in."

"Hold onto the life buoy and I'll get help," Conefluence said. True to his word, he returned in a couple of minutes, riding on the back of a small truck. "Hi, this truck has a winch and a rope on his bumper. We'll have Conerad out in no time." Conefluence unwound some rope and threw it to Conerad, who held on tightly.

The truck slowly wound up the rope. The four Cones took hold of Conerad and pulled him onto the bank. He coughed and spluttered. "I guess the lesson there is: don't walk on grass near a canal bank!" Conen said, thoughtfully. Conestance took a tissue out of her bag and wiped some slimy green weed off Conerad's face.

The sun was setting so the Cones took off their hi-viz coats and gave them back to Conefluence. "Thank you for a really interesting day. We now know how to be safe around water," they said. As Conefluence woggled away, they settled down for the night - Just Cones, no faces, no voices, no hands, no movements: Just Cones.

Wise Owl flew silently through the darkness, found Police car and landed on his blue lights. She told him about the Cones' day.

"I'm glad they had Coneﬂuence to help," Police Car said. "They've learned a lot today. We couldn't have got Conerad out of the water."

"Tooowooo Trooohooo," hooted Wise Owl. She spread her wings and flew away into the darkness.

The Cones have learned lots of lessons about being safe on rivers and canals. Have fun, but keep safe when *you* are near water.